A Heart for Ruby

FRANZESKA G. EWART

ILLUSTRATED BY

LAUREN TOBIA

WALKER BOOKS

For the children of
St Winning's Primary School, Kilwinning
F.G.E.

For Mum
L.T.

First published 2009 by Walker Books Ltd
87 Vauxhall Walk, London SE11 5HJ

4 6 8 10 9 7 5 3

Text © 2009 Franzeska G. Ewart
Illustrations © 2009 Lauren Tobia

The right of Franzeska G. Ewart and Lauren Tobia to be identified as author
and illustrator respectively of this work has been asserted by them in
accordance with the Copyright, Designs and Patents Act 1988

This book has been typeset in Bembo Educational
and Cochin-BoldItalic

Printed and bound in China

British Library Cataloguing in Publication Data:
a catalogue record for this book is available from the British Library

ISBN: 978-1-4063-0910-2

www.walker.co.uk

Lucky Mascots
5

A Heart for Ruby
25

Lighter than Air
45

Lucky
Mascots

It was Wednesday morning, and Ruby Rai stood in the gym hall clutching a red heart-shaped balloon to her chest.

Girls and boys danced all around her, and as Ruby watched them, she felt more and more miserable. They were all so much better than she was!

Sometimes they stood on tiptoe
and turned circles. Sometimes
they jumped in the air.

And as they turned
and jumped, they
waved their balloons
gracefully in time to
the music.

Ruby's heart
sank right down
to her toes.

When *she*
stood on
tiptoe and
turned circles,
she wobbled so
much she fell over.

When *she* jumped,
her feet hardly left
the ground.

And when *she* tried to wave her balloon gracefully, it got caught between her knees.

There are no two ways about it, Ruby thought sadly. I just can't dance!

"Come along, Ruby!" shouted Mrs Golightly. "Jump!"

Ruby gritted her teeth, took a little run, jumped … and landed with a huge **THUD!**

"You could be a bit lighter, Ruby,"
Mrs Golightly said gently. "Little
Lovehearts should be lighter than air."

After they had finished
the lesson, Mrs Golightly
told everyone to walk quietly
back to the classroom.

  "The Valentine's Day concert
is on Friday," she reminded them.
"Only a few days left to practise our
Loveheart Dance!"

Ruby leant over to her best friend, Rowan. "I'll never be lighter than air," she whispered. "Not by Friday, anyway."

"Course you will," Rowan whispered back.

"You just have to believe you can do it."

Rowan took something green and fluffy out of her pencil case. "My lucky mascot," she explained, handing it to Ruby. "Want to borrow it?"

Ruby stared at Rowan's fluffy mascot. "What is it?" she asked.

"It's a four-leaf clover," Rowan said. "It fits onto the end of my pencil.

My gran gave it to me," she added.
"She says four-leaf clovers are lucky.
And this one *always* brings me luck."

The bell rang for home time. Ruby
handed the four-leaf clover back to
Rowan. "Thanks ever so much,"
she said. "I might try it next time we
do Mental Maths."

Auntie Pooja was waiting in the playground. She was studying at college and lived with Mum and Ruby. Mum didn't finish work till late, so Auntie Pooja always collected Ruby from school.

18

It was snowing, so Ruby held Auntie Pooja's hand tight.

"Do you have a lucky mascot?" Ruby asked as they slithered along.

"I've got loads!" Auntie Pooja laughed. "Lucky rings, lucky necklaces—"

"And lucky earrings?"
Auntie Pooja nodded and
tucked her hair behind her ears.
She was wearing dangly
diamond earrings.

"These earrings
are one of my
luckiest pairs,"
she said as they
arrived home.
"I wore them
when I sat my
driving test –
and I passed!"

Inside, Auntie Pooja knelt down and lit the gas fire. Then she stood up and shook the snow from her hair. As her earrings swayed, they sent hundreds of tiny lights onto the walls. It looked as if the whole room was filled with bright, shiny raindrops. The shiny raindrops made Ruby feel all light and tingly inside.

"Perhaps," she said, "if I had a sparkly mascot, it would make me lighter than air…"

Auntie Pooja smiled. "Let's make my earrings sparkle even more!" And, laughing, she grabbed Ruby's hands and they danced round and round the room.

"After tea," Auntie Pooja said, "let's look in my jewellery box. There's bound to be a sparkly lucky mascot just for you."

Ruby was over the moon. A sparkly lucky mascot was *sure* to make her lighter than air!

A Heart
for Ruby

Ever since Rowan had shown her the fluffy four-leaf clover, Ruby just couldn't get mascots out of her head.

"Do you have a lucky mascot, Mum?" she asked after tea.

"I have a lucky hairdo!" Mum said.

"Whenever I want something to go extra-specially well," she went on, "I ask my friend at Krazy Kuts to do my hair."

She winked at Ruby. "She's giving me a funky Valentine's hairdo on Friday. So your dance is bound to be a success!"

Ruby said nothing. The thought of Mum's funky hairdo worried her. Supposing the Loveheart Dance wasn't a success?

Supposing she wobbled and fell? Or landed with a huge thud?

She tiptoed upstairs to Auntie Pooja's room. Her aunt was lying on the bed, reading.

"Can I come in?" Ruby asked.

"For a little while," said Auntie Pooja. "I have to study. Exam on Monday!"

She brought out her jewellery box
and opened it.

Ruby stirred the bright jumble of
jewellery round and round. She found
a pair of shiny blue earrings. They were
shaped like little tears. When she held
them up, tiny blue raindrops seemed to
fall on the walls.

"Those are lucky earrings,"
Auntie Pooja said. "I wore them to a
Bollywood dancing competition. They
went with my blue sari and my pointy
blue shoes."

Aunty Pooja put the earrings on.
Then she spun round, very fast. When
she spun, she kept her back straight.
She didn't wobble at all.

"Did you win?"
Ruby asked.
Auntie Pooja
nodded. "First
prize!"

Ruby stirred the bright jumble of jewellery round and round again. She found another pair of earrings. They were parrots, with shiny black eyes and emerald-green feathers. When she held them up, tiny green raindrops seemed to fall on the walls.

"Those are *very* lucky earrings,"
Auntie Pooja said. "I wore them to my
first netball match. They went with my
green skirt and stripy green socks."

She took off the blue earrings and
put on the green ones. Then she
jumped up, very high. When
Auntie Pooja landed, she
bent her knees. She
landed as softly
as snow.

"Did you win?" Ruby asked.

Auntie Pooja nodded.

"Top of the league!"

Ruby peered back into the jewellery box. She stirred round and round, but she could only find one more earring. It was heart-shaped, and covered with bright red stones. When Ruby held it up, tiny red raindrops seemed to fall on the walls.

Ruby thought it was the most beautiful earring she had ever seen, and she waited to hear how lucky it was.

But this time, Auntie Pooja had an unhappy story to tell.

"My granny gave me those earrings," she said. "Which makes them very special. But I never found out if they were lucky, because I lost one."

Ruby stroked the twinkling red heart. She thought it looked terribly lonely.

"I was dancing at a disco," Auntie Pooja went on. "Jumping very high and spinning very fast. One of them must have flown off. I never, ever found it."

She took the earring from Ruby.
"I wanted you to have these one day,"
Auntie Pooja said sadly. "Because
they're made of rubies."

Then she pinned the little red heart
onto Ruby's jumper — right above
her own heart!

"Your very own
sparkly lucky
mascot," Auntie
Pooja told Ruby.
"To bring you
luck with your
Loveheart
Dance."

Ruby peered down at the little ruby heart. It didn't look so lonely any more. And, though she couldn't see them, she knew her chin was covered with tiny red raindrops.

She was sure her sparkly mascot would bring her all the luck in the world!

Lighter than Air

45

On Thursday afternoon, when Ruby
trudged home through the snow with
Auntie Pooja, her heart glowed with
happiness.

The last Loveheart Dance practice
had gone really well.

As they had waited to start, Rowan had whispered to Ruby, "Remember, just believe you can do it!"

Ruby had nodded happily. With the ruby earring pinned to her T-shirt, she really did believe she could dance as well as anyone!

And she did. That afternoon, with those magical sparkles glistening on her chin, she felt as graceful as Auntie Pooja.

As Ruby began to dance, she just
knew she wouldn't wobble – and she
didn't. The more she danced, the more
she felt her steps becoming lighter and
lighter. Soon they were lighter than air
– just like Auntie Pooja's!

Mrs Golightly was delighted. "What
an improvement, Ruby," she said,
beaming. "You're a proper
little Loveheart
now!"

One thing,
however, still bothered
Ruby. If Auntie Pooja hadn't lost
the other ruby earring, she could
have worn them both to her exam on
Monday. They would have been sure
to bring her luck!

It was such a shame.

"I'm going to study for a bit," said Auntie Pooja when they arrived home, and she went upstairs.

Ruby flopped down on the settee and thought about the missing earring. She wished with all her heart that she could find it.

It had to be very lonely, all on its own somewhere.

Sadly, she began to practise her Loveheart Dance. Then she stopped. Somehow her heart just wasn't in it.

Unpinning the ruby heart from her jumper, she climbed the stairs. She knocked softly on Auntie Pooja's door.

"May I come in," she asked, "just for a minute?"

Auntie Pooja was sitting at her desk, surrounded by piles and piles of books.

Rather shyly,
Ruby held out the
ruby heart. "You
can have it,"
she told Auntie
Pooja. "To bring
you luck in your
exam…"

To Ruby's surprise,
Auntie Pooja
burst out laughing.
Then she gave her
a hug and a big
red kiss.

56

"What a sweetheart you are, Ruby!" she said. She picked up one of the thickest books and gave it a thump. "But I don't need a lucky mascot to pass my exam. All I need to do is study hard!"

She pinned the ruby heart back onto Ruby's chest. "Thank you very much," she said. "It was a lovely thought."

On Friday afternoon, everyone came
to the gym hall for the Valentine's Day
concert. Mum and Auntie Pooja sat in
the front row, both looking extremely
glamorous. Mum's hair had red-tipped

spikes; and Auntie Pooja's was piled
up like a chocolate twirl. Mum was
wearing a new red top, covered in
sequins; and Auntie Pooja was wearing
a bright pink sari.

When Ruby walked out, ready to start the Loveheart Dance, she was sure her ruby heart was sparkling twice as much as before.

The dance began. Everyone turned,
and jumped, and waved their balloons
gracefully. But no one danced as
gracefully as Ruby.

When she stood on tiptoe and turned, she kept her back straight. She hardly wobbled at all.

When she jumped, she soared into the
air; and when she landed, she bent her
knees. She landed as softly as snow.

As Ruby took her final bow, Auntie Pooja gave her a big wink.

Ruby winked back. And she was sure the ruby heart, twinkling on her chest, was winking too!